D0256399

Where teddy bears come from

PUFFIN

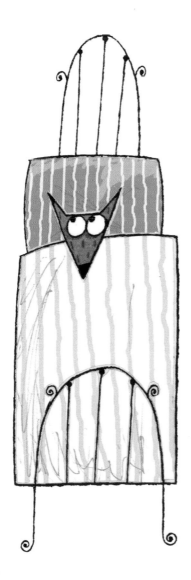

Written by
Mark Burgess

Illustrated by
Russell Ayto

In the middle of
a deep, dark forest,
all the creatures were fast asleep.
Except for a little grey wolf
who tossed and turned
and couldn't sleep a wink.

Mother Wolf
gave the little wolf a
glass of milk
and a **cuddle**.

Then she tucked him up tight
and read his favourite
teddy bear story
three times over.

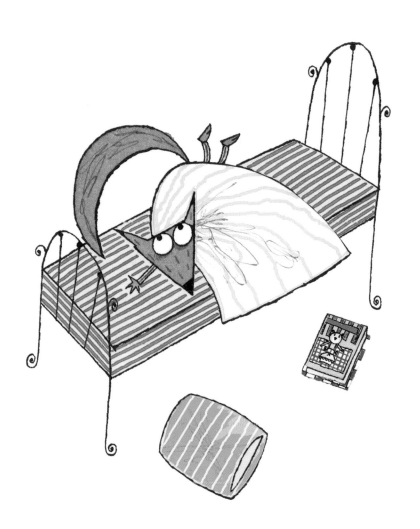

But it was no good.

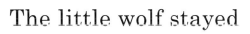
The little wolf stayed

wide awake . . .

Until, at last, the morning sun peeped in.

The sunlight shone on a picture in his storybook.

"That's what I need!" cried the little wolf.

"A teddy bear! That will help me sleep!"

"Where do teddy bears come from?"

the little wolf asked his mother.

But Mother Wolf didn't know. "Why don't you ask Wise Owl?" she said.

"Wise Owl knows everything."

"Yes, I will," said the little wolf bravely,

for though he was rather shy, he very much wanted a teddy bear.

Mother Wolf
packed a picnic.
"Be careful and be
sure to be back by
bedtime," she said,
and the little wolf set
off through the forest
to find Wise Owl.

Wise Owl
was fast asleep.

"Please," whispered the little wolf.
"Where do teddy bears come from?
I can't sleep and I need a teddy bear."

Wise Owl opened one eye. "Hmm," he muttered,
"I usually have no trouble sleeping."
He opened the other eye.
"And I don't know much about bears, especially teddy bears.
Perhaps you should ask the Three Little Pigs?"

So the little wolf thanked him and set off through the forest.

After a while,
the little wolf came to a little
brick house beside a stream.

"The Three Little Pigs must
live here," said the little wolf.
"If I ask politely, they're sure
to tell me about teddy bears."

But as the shy little wolf
approached the house,
his nose began to *twitch*,
and tickle,
until . . .

"A . . . A . . .

Three not-so-little pigs ran out of the cottage.

"Why, if it isn't a wolf!" cried the first pig.
"Shoo, you bad wolf, shoo!"
cried the second pig.
"Go back to the forest right now,"
cried the third pig,
"or we'll have your hide for a handbag!"

"No, **no, no!**" cried the little wolf.
"I'm not **the bad wolf.**"

The three not-so-little pigs peered down at him.
"No, you're not **the bad wolf,**" they said,
"but if you don't want to **huff** and **puff**
and **blow our house down**, what do you want?"

"Please," said the little wolf.
"Where do teddy bears come from?
I can't sleep and I need a teddy bear."

"Oh!" said the third pig. "But we don't know anything about teddy bears.
We sing lullabies to get to sleep."
And the three not-so-little pigs nodded in agreement.
"Perhaps you should ask Little Red Riding Hood."

So the little wolf thanked them and went on through the forest.

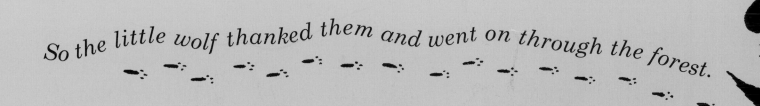

After a while, the little wolf
came to a pretty thatched cottage.

"This cottage looks very friendly,"
said the little wolf to himself.
"This time I will be brave and knock.
I'm sure Little Red Riding Hood
knows all about teddy bears."

The little wolf hurried up
to the front door, but his claws
were rather long and he
tripped over the doormat . . . .

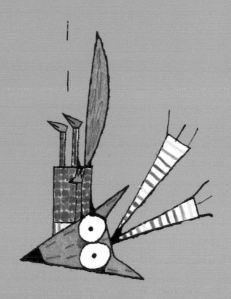

CRASH!

And

landed

in the

laundry

basket.

A girl in a scarlet cloak
ran into the hallway.
"Why, if it isn't a wolf!" she cried.
"Shoo, you big bad wolf, shoo!
You just go back to the forest this very
minute or we'll have your hide for a hearth rug!"

"NO, NO, NO!" cried the little wolf.
"I'm not the big bad wolf."

"Well," said the little girl crossly,
"if you're not the big bad wolf and you
don't want to gobble us up, what do you want?"

"Please," said the little wolf.
"Where do teddy bears come from?
I can't sleep and I need a teddy bear."

"Oh!" said the girl. "Well, we don't bother with teddy bears.
We count sheep to get to sleep."
And the girl and her grandma nodded in agreement.
"Perhaps you should ask Goldilocks.
She knows about bears."

So the little wolf thanked them and went on through the forest.

By now, the little wolf was very tired.
He wandered along, not looking where he was going,
which was how he bumped into an old man who
was bending down beside a big red truck.

"Why, if it isn't a wolf!"
cried the rosy-faced old man.

The little wolf scrabbled to his feet.

"But I'm not the
big bad wolf!" he shouted.

"Well, that is a shame,"
said the old man,
"because I need someone with a bit of
puff to blow this tyre up."

"Oh, well, in that case I could
have a try," said the little wolf.

So he huffed . . .

and he
puffed . . .

and he huffed
and he puffed
and he blew the tyre up . . .
and up . . .

"STOP!!" cried the old man.
"That will do nicely, thank you.
Now then, little wolf, one good turn
deserves another so what can I do for you?"

"Please," said the little wolf.
"Where do teddy bears
come from?
I can't sleep and I need a teddy bear."

The old man nodded in agreement.
"Ho, ho, ho!" he said.
"Where do teddy bears come from?
What a question!
If you run home right now, I promise that
you'll have the answer in the morning."

"Oh, thank you!" cried the little wolf
and he ran all the way home.

That night, the little wolf
didn't need a glass of milk,
or a story, or a cuddle.

He was so tired he fell
fast asleep at once and slept
the whole night through.

In the morning there was an odd-shaped parcel
at the bottom of his bed.

The little wolf could hardly believe his eyes.

Inside the parcel was the **softest**, **cuddliest** teddy bear anyone could wish for. The little wolf hugged his teddy tightly and quickly ran outside.

"Now I know where
teddy bears
come from!" he cried.

Ever after the little wolf had no trouble sleeping.

*And that might not be where all teddy bears come from,
but it's where one little wolf got his.*

For
Rosie
   – M. B.
For those
  who believe
    – R. A.

PUFFIN BOOKS
Published by the Penguin Group:

London, New York, Australia, Canada, India,
Ireland, New Zealand and South Africa

Penguin Books Ltd,
Registered Offices: 80 Strand,

London WC2R 0RL, England
puffinbooks.com

First published 2008
1 2 3 4 5 6 7 8 9 10

Text copyright © Mark Burgess, 2008
Illustrations copyright © Russell Ayto, 2008
All rights reserved

The moral right of the author and
illustrator has been asserted

Printed in China
ISBN: 978–0–141–50046–1